Olive's Perfect World

Olive's Perfect World

A Friendship Story

Jennifer Plecas

PHILOMEL BOOKS ✱ An Imprint of Penguin Group (USA) Inc.

To SFK

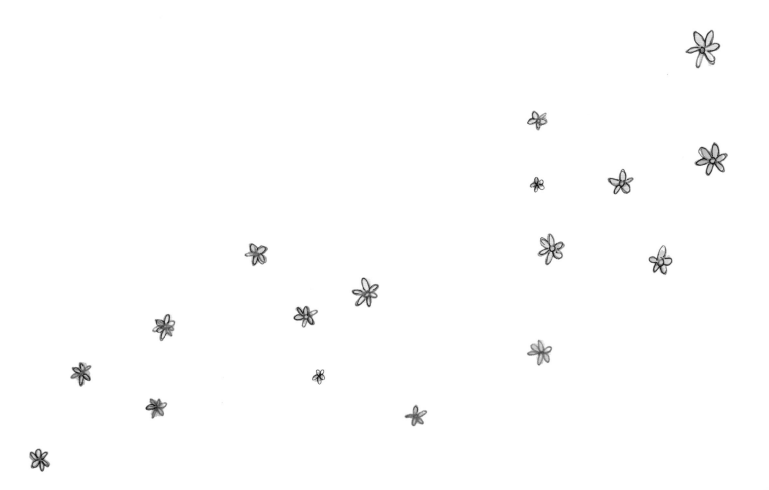

Olive and Emily were friends.

Olive and Emily had always been friends—ever since they both could remember.

In Olive's perfect world, it was Olive and Emily, friends from the beginning doing everything together, and friends forever.

Period.

The end.

But in the real world, lately, there was

Olive and Emily and also . . .

. . . Eva.

This might have been okay, except that Eva seemed to care only about Emily. It was as if Olive was invisible.

Worse, it was starting to feel like Emily and Eva were the real friends and Olive was just . . . plain Olive.

All by herself.

It got even worse when Emily and Eva started dance class together.

In Olive's perfect world, leaping around and doing ballet together didn't make people friends.

Emily and Eva started planning to
wear the same things on the same
day. Like matching bows.

Or nail polish.

Or their matching ballet T-shirts, which
were an ugly throw-up purple color. It made
Olive sick to see it—even out of the corner of
her eye.

In Olive's perfect world, there was no ugly throw-up purple color. And matching didn't make friends. Being friends made people friends.

Olive noticed other things, too.

Emily and Eva started calling each other "the Sparkle-Es,"
because both of their names started with the letter E.

Not much later they each got the same exact lunch bag.

And to top it off, they found that they brought the same exact kind of applesauce for lunch.

"Oh my gosh, we're LUNCH TWINS!" Eva said.

"And APPLESAUCE TWINS!" Emily said.

"Hey, we're—APPLESAUCE-GRAPE TWINS!" Olive said, holding up a grape.

"That doesn't make any sense," said Eva.

"Well, maybe not to you," Olive said.

Emily laughed. "I like applesauce-grape twins!" she said, smiling at Olive.

In Olive's perfect world, your name didn't have to start with the same letter to be friends with someone. And everyone knew that twins meant that you were born at the same time, not that you had the same lunch bag or applesauce.

Olive watched for the ten thousandth time as Emily
and Eva practiced their ballet routine.

"Hey," Olive said, "do you guys want to do the chicken dance?"

Olive flapped her arms and wiggled her hips, humming the tune.

"We need to practice this," Emily said.

"What kind of dance is the chicken dance?" Eva said.

"A good one," Olive said. "Emily and I used to do it all the time—remember?"

"Yes," Emily said. "It is a good one."

But Emily and Eva didn't want to do the chicken dance.

In Olive's perfect world, friends liked to do the fun things you used to do together. And paid attention to you. And noticed when you felt all crumpled up and soggy, instead of ignoring you and practicing tutu twirls.

Over and over and over again.

Olive and Emily were friends.

But Olive wasn't sure if Emily knew this.

Because it was Eva and Emily who: Matched every day.
Did ballet together. Called themselves "the Sparkle-Es."
Were Lunch Twins. And Applesauce Twins.

And now—Spot Sisters. Because they both had spots.

"You probably didn't realize," Olive said,

"but I'm a Spot Sister, too!"

"But you're striped!" said Eva.

"Mostly," Olive said, "but look. My paws."

"I think your spots are smearing," Eva said.

"I was just kidding," Olive said quickly.

In Olive's perfect world, she was just kidding.

But in the real world, water began to fill Olive's eyes, and before she could even blink, a big tear rolled down her face.

"Olive," Emily said, "are you crying?"

No words could get past the lump in Olive's throat.

"You can be a Spot Sister, too!" Emily said.

"Yes," said Eva, "you can be a Spot Sister, Olive!"

"I don't want to be a Spot Sister," Olive managed to say. And she meant it.

Olive didn't want to be a Spot Sister. Or a Sparkle-E or an Applesauce Twin or any of those things.

She just wanted to be Emily's friend. Like before.

"It's just . . . ," Olive said. "It's just that you guys have everything together now. And I'm . . . I'm just plain Olive."

"You're not plain, Olive!" Emily said.

"I think you're more chocolate chip than plain!" said Eva.

Olive laughed a little.

Emily and Eva laughed, too.

"I'm strawberry!" Emily said.

"And I'm mint!" said Eva.

"Or maybe we're all rainbow sherbet!" Emily said.

"To rainbow sherbet!" Eva said.

Olive, Emily, and Eva all laughed. "To rainbow sherbet!" they said.

And Olive felt a small warm spot where the twisted-up lump in her stomach had been lately. It felt good.

"Hey," Emily said, "this feels like the perfect
time for the chicken dance!"

"Cluck, cluck!" said Eva. "Show me this thing!"

Emily started to hum the tune, and soon Olive and Emily were doing the chicken dance. Just like always.

Eva joined in, and then they were all dancing together.

Olive flapped her wings and wiggled her hips.

She, Emily, and Eva all knocked elbows and bumped into each other as they danced. Eva got the tune wrong a few times.

In Olive's perfect world, people didn't mess up the tune or bump into each other when they danced.

Or did they?

Because right then, doing the chicken dance and laughing with friends felt pretty . . .

. . . perfect.

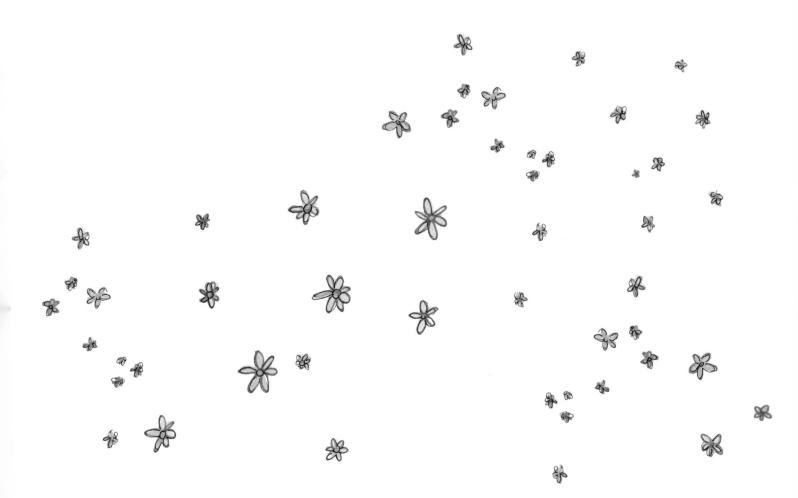

PHILOMEL BOOKS
A division of Penguin Young Readers Group.   Published by The Penguin Group.
Penguin Group (USA) Inc., 375 Hudson Street, New York, NY 10014, U.S.A.
Penguin Group (Canada), 90 Eglinton Avenue East, Suite 700, Toronto, Ontario M4P 2Y3, Canada (a division of Pearson Penguin Canada Inc.).
Penguin Books Ltd, 80 Strand, London WC2R 0RL, England.
Penguin Ireland, 25 St. Stephen's Green, Dublin 2, Ireland (a division of Penguin Books Ltd).
Penguin Group (Australia), 707 Collins Street, Melbourne, Victoria 3008, Australia (a division of Pearson Australia Group Pty Ltd).
Penguin Books India Pvt Ltd, 11 Community Centre, Panchsheel Park, New Delhi - 110 017, India.
Penguin Group (NZ), 67 Apollo Drive, Rosedale, Auckland 0632, New Zealand (a division of Pearson New Zealand Ltd).
Penguin Books South Africa, Rosebank Office Park, 181 Jan Smuts Avenue, Parktown North 2193, South Africa.
Penguin China, B7 Jiaming Center, 27 East Third Ring Road North, Chaoyang District, Beijing 100020, China.
Penguin Books Ltd, Registered Offices: 80 Strand, London WC2R 0RL, England.

Copyright © 2013 by Jennifer Plecas.

Edited by Jill Santopolo.   Design by Semadar Megged.
Text set in 15-point Johnston ITC Light.   The illustrations were done in pen and ink and watercolor.
Library of Congress Cataloging-in-Publication Data
Plecas, Jennifer. Olive's perfect world / Jennifer Plecas. p. cm. Summary: In Olive's perfect world, she and Emily do everything together
and are friends forever, but in the real world, Eva is becoming Emily's friend, too, and Olive feels left out.
[1. Friendship—Fiction.] I. Title. PZ7.P7173Oli 2013 [E]—dc23 2012028563
ISBN 978-0-399-25287-7   10 9 8 7 6 5 4 3 2 1

ALWAYS LEARNING   PEARSON